Gettysburg Address

Written by Douglas M. Rife

Illustrated by Bron Smith

Teaching & Learning Company

1204 Buchanan St., P.O. Box 10
Carthage, IL 62321-0010

This book belongs to

_____

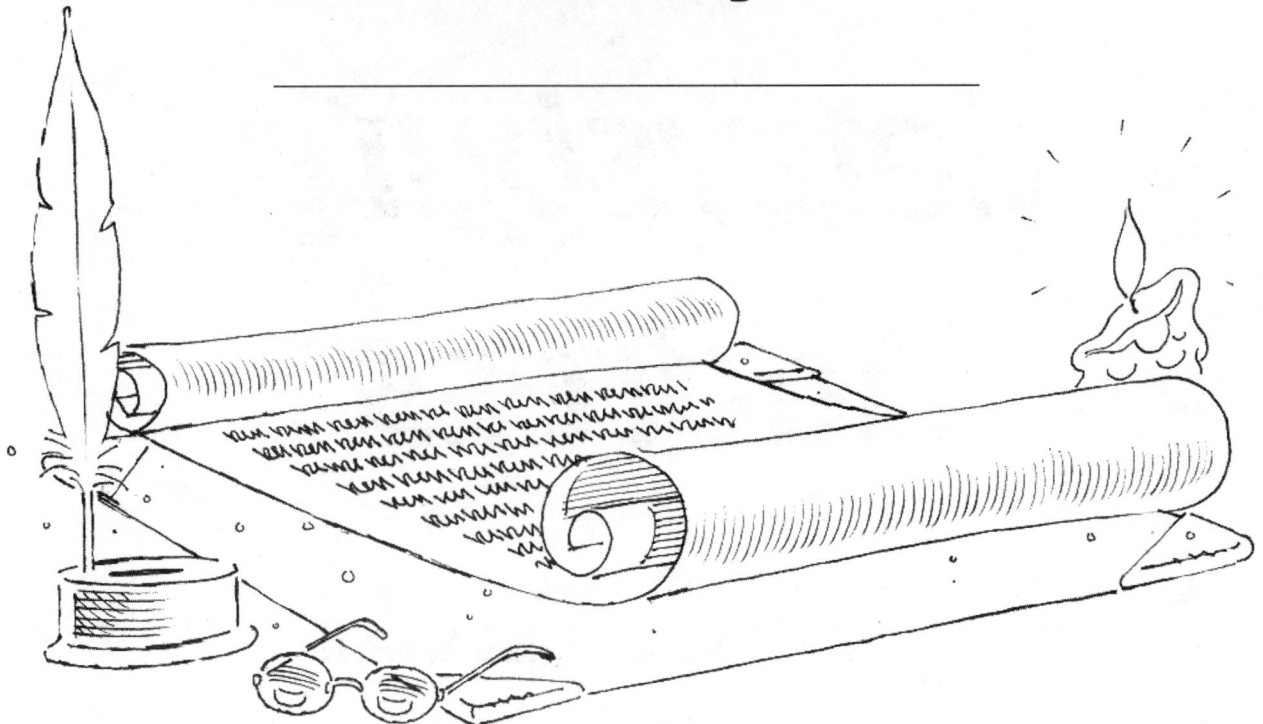

The photograph on the cover was taken by Alexander Gardner in his Washington, D.C., studio four days before Lincoln delivered the Gettysburg Address on November 19, 1863.

Cover photo obtained from the Photoduplication Service of the Library of Congress.

Copyright © 1997, Teaching & Learning Company

ISBN No. 1-57310-078-1

Printing No. 98765

Teaching & Learning Company
1204 Buchanan St., P.O. Box 10
Carthage, IL 62321-0010

The purchase of this book entitles teachers to make copies for use in their individual classrooms only. This book, or any part of it, may not be reproduced in any form for any other purposes without prior written permission from the Teaching & Learning Company. It is strictly prohibited to reproduce any part of this book for an entire school or school district, or for commercial resale.

All rights reserved. Printed in the United States of America.

Table of Contents

Objectives 5
Abraham Lincoln Biography   Handout 1 6
Biography Crossword   Handout 2 12
The Civil War   Handout 3 13
Civil War Time Line   Handout 4 16
Battle of Gettysburg   Handout 5 17
Battle of Gettysburg Map   Handout 6 21
Handwritten Version of Gettysburg Address   Handout 7   22
Gettysburg Address   Handout 8 23
Understanding the Gettysburg Address   Handout 9 24
Newspaper and Personal Accounts   Handout 10 25
Understanding the Newspaper and Personal Accounts
    Handout 11 26
Political Cartoons   Handout 12 27
Understanding the Cartoon   Handout 13 28
Bibliography 29
Answer Key 30

Dear Teacher or Parent,

The Gettysburg Address is one of the most important speeches in American history. The study of the speech provides an opportunity to focus on the Battle of Gettysburg, considered by many historians to be a significant turning point in the Civil War. Edward Everett, a popular orator of the time, wrote to Lincoln afterwards, "I should be glad if I could flatter myself that I came as near to the central idea of the occasion in two hours as you did in two minutes." Abraham Lincoln's plain, powerful words that day in November still speak to us today.

The Gettysburg Address is one of the most eloquent arguments in history for American democracy. Lincoln clearly continues the main and most important theme of the Declaration of Independence which declares, "all men are created equal," while boldly expanding that statement to include slaves.

The study of the Gettysburg Address is also a good way to introduce young history students to primary source documents. This reproducible book provides activities for students to investigate an important American speech, as well as place it in the larger context of events that led to its writing.

The six activities in this unit have two parts—narrative and review. Students first read the narratives and then review the material through a variety of activities, including crossword puzzles, mapping activities, time lines, and questions and answers that test for comprehension and understanding. The activities are designed to work together as one unit but may also be used alone.

Sincerely,

Douglas M. Rife

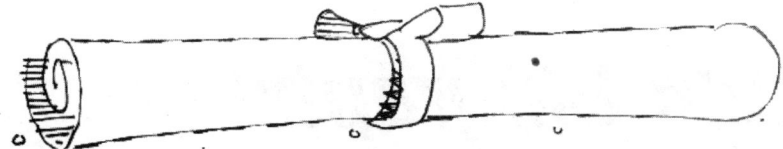

Objectives

After completing the following activities	the students should be able to . . .
Abraham Lincoln Biography	List the following characteristics of Abraham Lincoln: • love of learning • sense of humor • ability to keep trying • commitment to saving the Union
The Civil War	1. list the reasons for the Civil War 2. list the events that led to the Civil War 3. identify the northern, southern and border states on a map
Battle of Gettysburg	1. describe the battle 2. explain the importance of the battle in political and military terms 3. diagram the battle
Gettysburg Address	1. put the address in historical perspective 2. synthesize the speech in their own words 3. describe Lincoln's political message 4. explain Lincoln's references to the Declaration of Independence
Newspaper Accounts	1. identify differing opinions 2. explain possible motivations of editorial writers 3. critique editorials 4. write editorials, pro and con
Political Cartoons	1. identify the political figures 2. interpret the political figures 3. explain symbolism 4. draw own cartoons

Abraham Lincoln Biography

Highlights of Abraham Lincoln's Life and Career

Born: February 12, 1809

Parents: Thomas and Nancy Hanks Lincoln

Birthplace: Hodgenville, Hardin County, Kentucky

Education: Self-educated

Religious Affiliation: None

Married: Mary Todd (1818-1882), November 4, 1842

Children: Robert Todd (1843-1926)
Edward Baker (1846-1850)
William Wallace (1850-1862)
Thomas "Tad" (1853-1871)

Military: Served in the Black Hawk War

Occupation: Lawyer, admitted to the bar in 1836

Nicknames: Honest Abe, Long Abe, Illinois Rail Splitter, Giant Killer

Political Parties: Whig, Republican

Political Bids: 1832–lost race for a seat in the Illinois House of Representatives
1833–appointed postmaster, New Salem, Illinois
1834–elected to the Illinois legislature
1846–elected to one term in the U.S. House of Representatives
1855–lost U.S. Senate race
1856–lost bid for the Republican vice presidential nomination
1858–lost bid for for the U.S. Senate
1860–elected President
1864–reelected President

Died: April 15, 1865

Cause of Death: Assassinated from a gunshot to the head

Place of Death: Washington, D.C.

Buried: Oak Ridge Cemetery, Springfield, Illinois

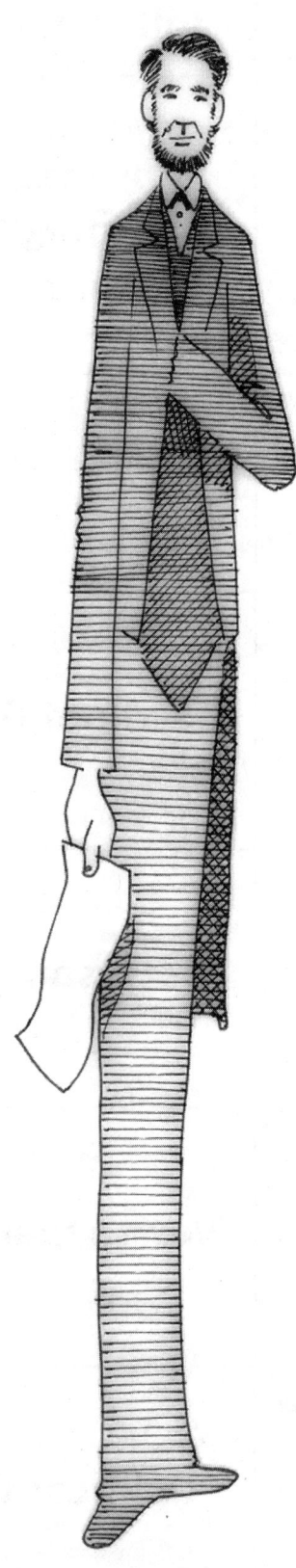

Lincoln's Presidential Election Returns

	Electoral Vote	Popular Vote
1860		
Abraham Lincoln (Republican)	180	1,866,452
John Breckinridge (Southern Democrat)	72	847,953
John Bell (Constitutional Union)	39	590,631
Stephen A. Douglas (Democrat)	12	1,375,157
1864		
Abraham Lincoln (Republican)	212	2,213,665
George Brinton McCellan (Democrat)	21	1,805,237

(The states of the Confederacy did not vote.)

Lincoln's Administration

Vice President

Hannibal Hamlin, 1861-1865
Andrew Johnson, 1865

Cabinet Members

Secretary of State
William H. Seward

Secretary of the Treasury
Salmon P. Chase, 1861-1864
William P. Fessenden, 1864-1865
Hugh McCulloch, 1865

Secretary of War
Simon Cameron, 1861-1862
Edwin M. Stanton, 1862-1865

Secretary of the Navy
Gideon Welles

Attorney General
Edward Bates, 1861-1864
James Speed, 1864-1865

Postmaster General
Montgomery Blair, 1861-1864
William Dennison, 1864-1865

Secretary of the Interior
Caleb B. Smith, 1861-1863
John P. Usher, 1863-1865

Abraham Lincoln was born in a log cabin in rural Kentucky in 1809. He grew up living on farms in both rural Kentucky and Indiana. His father and mother, Thomas and Nancy Hanks Lincoln, had two children, Sarah and Abraham. Lincoln's mother died when he was nine. His father's second wife, Sarah Bush Johnston, had three children of her own from a previous marriage. Lincoln became very close to his stepmother, who encouraged young Abe to study.

Lincoln preferred reading to farm work. Stories of Lincoln walking for miles to borrow a book have become legendary. Though one of Lincoln's favorite pastimes was reading, he still had to work on his father's farm. Abe was a tall, strong young man, who gained a reputation at a young age for chopping wood and splitting rails. The Illinois Rail Splitter nickname stuck with him throughout his political career.

Lincoln studied the law while he was working as a store clerk in New Salem, Illinois. He was admitted to the Illinois State Bar in 1836. Lincoln was civic minded and had always been interested in politics. He ran for a seat in the Illinois legislature in 1832 but lost. Lincoln's political career had many more ups and downs. He won and lost a series of elections in the 1830s, 40s and 50s. The race that gave him national acclaim and recognition was his unsuccessful bid, in 1858, for the U.S. Senate seat against Stephen A. Douglas, nicknamed the "Little Giant." Though he lost, Lincoln gained fame as a speaker during a series of seven debates held throughout Illinois.

Lincoln was over six feet four inches tall and some described him as homely. After he became the Republican nominee for the presidency, the Houston Telegraph wrote, "Lincoln is the leanest, lankest, most ungainly mass of legs and arms and hatchet face ever strung on a single frame. He has most unwarrantly abused the privilege, which all politicians have, of being ugly." Contrasted against the short, robust Stephen Douglas, who stood five feet four inches tall, Lincoln looked gangly and awkward. His sense of humor, however, allowed him to poke fun at himself. During one of their debates, Douglas accused Lincoln of being two-faced. Lincoln retorted, "If I had another face, do you think I'd wear this one?"

Though Lincoln lost to the "Little Giant," he gained a national reputation. It was during those debates that Lincoln said, "A house divided against itself cannot stand." Two years later, in 1860, Lincoln won the Republican nomination as presidential standard bearer. The Democrats split. John Breckinridge ran as a Southern Democrat, Stephen Douglas as a Northern Democrat. Once again, Stephen Douglas and Abraham Lincoln ran against each other in an election. This time, after a contentious election, Lincoln won. He also won another nickname—Giant Killer—because he had defeated Stephen Douglas, the Little Giant, and won the most important elected office in the United States.

Shortly after Lincoln won the presidential election, southern states started seceding from the Union. South Carolina was the first state to withdraw, but others soon followed. By the time Abraham Lincoln took the oath of office on March 4, 1861, the southern states had formed a separate government, the Confederate States of America. On April 12, 1861, a shot was fired against Fort Sumter, South Carolina, and the Civil War had begun. Lincoln set about saving the Union.

Though many believed the war would be over quickly; it lasted from 1861-1865. During that time, Lincoln directed much of the war and managed to be reelected for a second term in 1864. In 1862, during his first term, Lincoln suffered great personal tragedy when his son Willie died. Lincoln suffered from long periods of depression and melancholy. In January 1863, Lincoln issued the Emancipation Proclamation which freed the slaves. He believed that if he were to be remembered by history, it would be for the act alone. On November 19, that same year, Lincoln gave his now famous Gettysburg Address to dedicate the Soldier's Cemetery in Gettysburg, Pennsylvania.

Lincoln's legacy was a preserved Union and the Emancipation Proclamation. Lincoln is considered one of the greatest American Presidents because of his unanswering devotion to save the nation born during the American Revolution and unshackle the bonds of slavery.

Handout 1

Name _____

Biography Crossword

Most of the clues and answers are about Lincoln, people and events from the Civil War period. Be careful, though, because there are a few general knowledge clues and answers. Don't let them trick you!

Across

1. Lincoln's party
7. Honest _____
8. _____ cabin
10. Domiciled animal
11. Its capital is Nashville (initials)
13. Walt Whitman's profession
14. Region below the Mason Dixon Line
16. Bigger than a town
17. Small _____ a mouse
19. Lawyers and the IRS work on this (two words)
23. Short for *Abraham*
24. Ford's _____
25. Mining product
26. One of Abe's favorite pastimes

Down

1. Woodchopper synonym (two words)
2. Author of *Charlotte's Web* (first initials)
3. Government of, by and for the _____
4. John Wilkes _____
5. Lincoln-Douglas debates' state
6. Johnson's birth state (initials)
9. Has a famous address
12. New Hampshire (abbreviation)
14. State of Civil War's first shot (initials)
15. Honeybee state (initials)
17. Rail splitter's tool
18. "As I would not be a _____, so I would not be a master"
20. First Secretary of State (initials)
21. A preposition
22. Unwanted garden plant
25. *Off*'s opposite

12   Handout 2   TLC10078 Copyright © Teaching & Learning Company, Carthage, IL 62321-0010

The Civil War

The slave trade began in the colonies almost as soon as Europeans settled on American shores. The practice began as a way to provide inexpensive labor and grew into an institution in the labor-intensive, agrarian South. Nevertheless, slavery was debated nearly from its beginning. Many Southerners who owned slaves questioned the institution of slavery while writing the Constitution of the United States. The Constitution, in fact, outlawed the foreign slave trade after the year 1808.

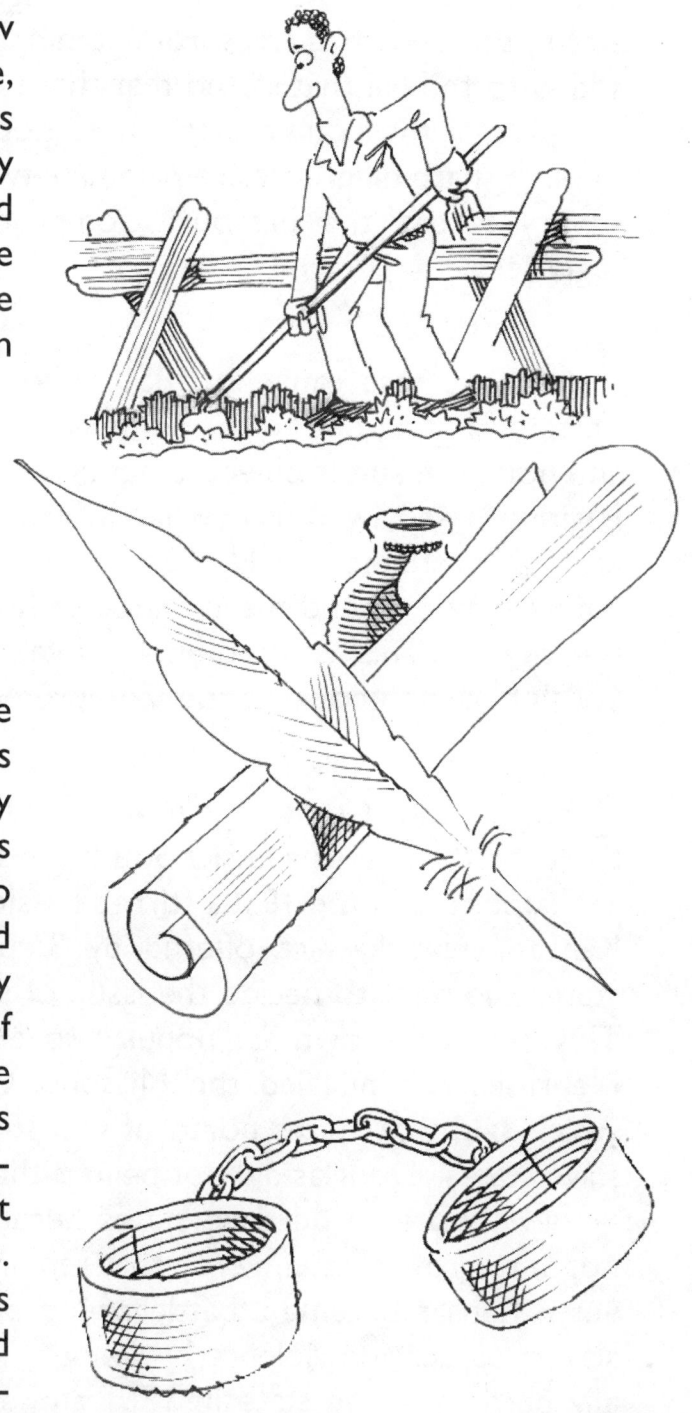

However, the constitutional ban on the importation of slaves from foreign countries did not end the debate. Slaves were illegally imported into the United States, and babies born to slaves therefore were born into slavery. Generations of slaves were traded and sold as property at auctions. Many Southerners argued that the institution of slavery was to be governed by the states—that it was, in fact, a state's rights issue. They argued that the federal government had no right to decide whether or not slavery existed in the individual states. Northerners argued that the institution was corrupt and that people should not be sold as property. The national debate over slavery, in part, shaped domestic policy in the United States.

Handout 3

The first great compromise between the pro-slavery and the anti-slavery factions came in 1820. The Missouri Territory had petitioned to become a state. By becoming a state, Missouri would upset the balance between free and slave states—there were 11 free states and 11 slave states in the Union. A compromise was agreed upon, Missouri could be added as a state at the same time as Maine. That would add one slave state and one free state to the Union, not changing the balance. In an attempt to keep this crisis from coming up again, language was added to the bill that stated that there could be no slavery in any part of the Louisiana Purchase north of the 36 30' line. Though sharp differences remained between the pro- and anti-slavery forces, the Missouri Compromise kept the Union together.

The next test came in 1850, when the southern states objected but agreed to the admission of California as a state, and northern states objected but agreed to the passage of the Fugitive Slave Law. This new law which promised that the federal government would help return runaway slaves and enforce laws to end the practice of helping slaves escape to the north. This compromise between the North and the South became known as the Compromise of 1850.

Though the Compromise of 1850 settled the dispute between the North and the South for a time, other events in the later part of the 1850s stirred passions about slavery. The Kansas-Nebraska Act, offered by Stephen A. Douglas, gave states the right to decide the issue of slavery for themselves. This became known as "popular sovereignty." The Kansas-Nebraska Act nullified the Missouri Compromise of 1820, which said that states north of the 36 30' line could not be slave states. Douglas did not believe that Nebraska or Kansas would choose to be slave states because they were too far north to grow cotton, a crop that required heavy labor to harvest. Kansas became a battleground between pro- and anti-slavery forces and violence broke out. Though Kansas eventually became a free state in 1861 and adopted a constitution that outlawed slavery, it also outlawed free blacks from living in the state.

The Supreme Court handed down a decision in the Dred Scott Case in 1857. Dred Scott was a slave who had traveled into several "free" states and territories with his owner. When his owner died, Scott sued in federal court for his freedom. The court ruled that slaves were not citizens, but property, and therefore had no rights. The court also said that slavery could not be banned by Congress or territorial legislatures. The decision further divided the country. Southerners saw the decision as a way to save the institution of slavery, and Northerners believed that the decision was wrong and should be overturned.

Shortly after Abraham Lincoln won the presidential election, southern states started seceding from the Union. South Carolina was the first state to withdraw and others soon followed. By February 1, 1861, seven states had seceded–South Carolina, Mississippi, Florida, Alabama, Georgia, Louisiana and Texas. By the time Abraham Lincoln took the oath of office on March 4, 1861, the southern states had formed a separate government–the Confederate States of America, with a capital in Montgomery, Alabama, and a president, Jefferson Davis.

On April 12, 1861, the first shot in the Civil War was fired against Fort Sumter, South Carolina. The fort was captured by Confederate forces. Though no soldiers on either side were killed that day, the Civil War had begun.

Name _____

Civil War Time Line

Place the following events on the time line next to the year in which they occurred.
(Note: Two of the events happened in the same year. Be careful to get them in the correct order.)

South Carolina secedes
Dred Scott decision
Lincoln elected
Compromise of 1850

Constitution outlaws foreign slave trade
Kansas-Nebraska Act
Missouri Compromise
Fort Sumter fired on

1808– _____

1820– _____

1850– _____

1854– _____

1857– _____

1860– _____

1861– _____

1861– _____

Battle of Gettysburg

The Southern forces, led by Robert E. Lee, were moving through Pennsylvania on the offensive—taking the war to the North. Lee believed Confederate troops in the North would draw out the Union Army and, once engaged in battle, his army would strike a fatal blow to the Army of the Potomac. Lee carried a letter from Confederate President Jefferson Davis authorizing a peace agreement.

Ironically, the Confederate Army was traveling south, and the Union Army, led by General George Meade, was traveling north when both armies converged on Gettysburg, Pennsylvania. For three days—July 1, 2 and 3— the two great armies battled.

The Battle of Gettysburg is extremely important because it was a turning point in the Civil War. Eighty to 85,000 northern troops and nearly 75,000 southern troops eventually converged on Gettysburg. The Battle of Gettysburg turned the tide for the North. The North suffered 23,000 casualties; the South, 20,000. Even though the losses were actually heavier on the northern side, the North held the high ground and won the three-day battle.

Handout 5

July 1

Union and Confederate forces converged on Gettysburg. Confederate troops, led by Major General Henry Heth, were gathered along Herr Ridge and Oak Hill, west of the little town. Union forces, led by Brigadier General John Burford, were lined up from the Hagerstown Road north along McPherson Ridge. These first troops to arrive at Gettysburg battled to gain the higher ground. The Confederate troops attacked the Union line around 9:00 in the morning. The Union line held. Rested northern troops arrived from the south. The Rebels attacked again a few hours later and still Union forces held. Confederate reinforcements began arriving as well. The Confederates attacked again in the afternoon, pushing the Union forces back. The Union forces retreated back through the town of Gettysburg and began to set up a defensive line. The first day had gone to the Confederate Army.

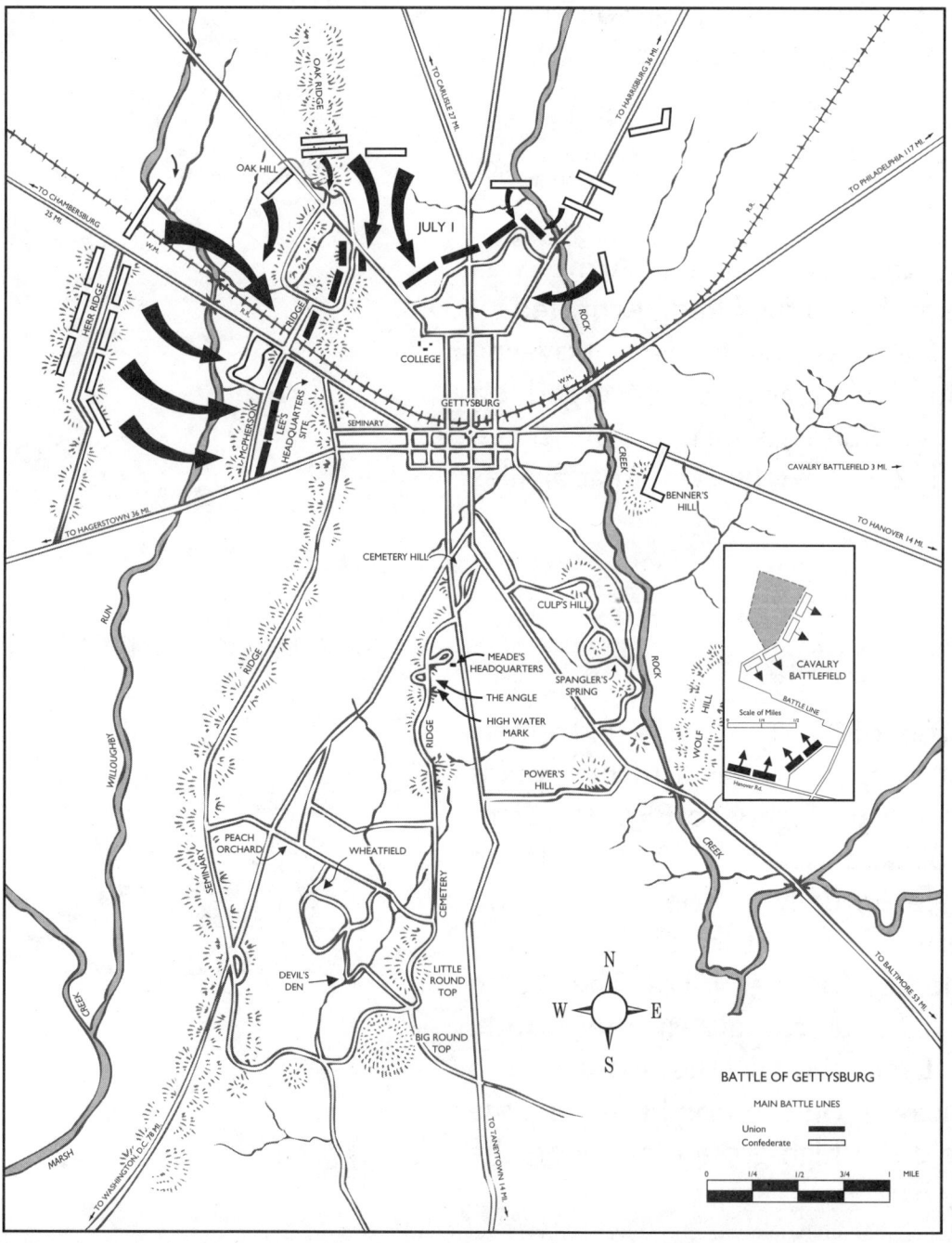

July 2

By the morning of July 2, the federal troops had set up a line in what has been described as an "upside-down fish hook." It began in the south at Little Round Top and stretched north along Cemetery Ridge, around Cemetery Hill, over Culp's Hill and down to Spangler's Spring. Troops under the command of Union Major General Daniel Sickles had moved forward from their positions along Cemetery Ridge forming a semicircle running north from Devil's Den to ground past the Peach Orchard. The Confederate forces were massed along Seminary Ridge as far north as the Chambersburg Road with another line of troops, led by Lieutenant General Richard Ewell, that faced Culp's Hill. The Confederate attack, led by General Longstreet, began late in the day. It had taken Longstreet most of the day to gather his troops and ready them for the battle. Longstreet believed it was a bad idea to attack the Union troops on this ground. He thought the Rebel troops should maneuver around the Union Army and fight them somewhere else. Lee ordered the attack. The casualties were heavy on both sides. The Confederates pushed back the southern part of the "fish hook" but did not break through the Union line or take Little Round Top. The Union troops had fallen back to Cemetery Ridge and held the ground. Ewell's attack on Culp's Hill and Cemetery Hill had not been successful either.

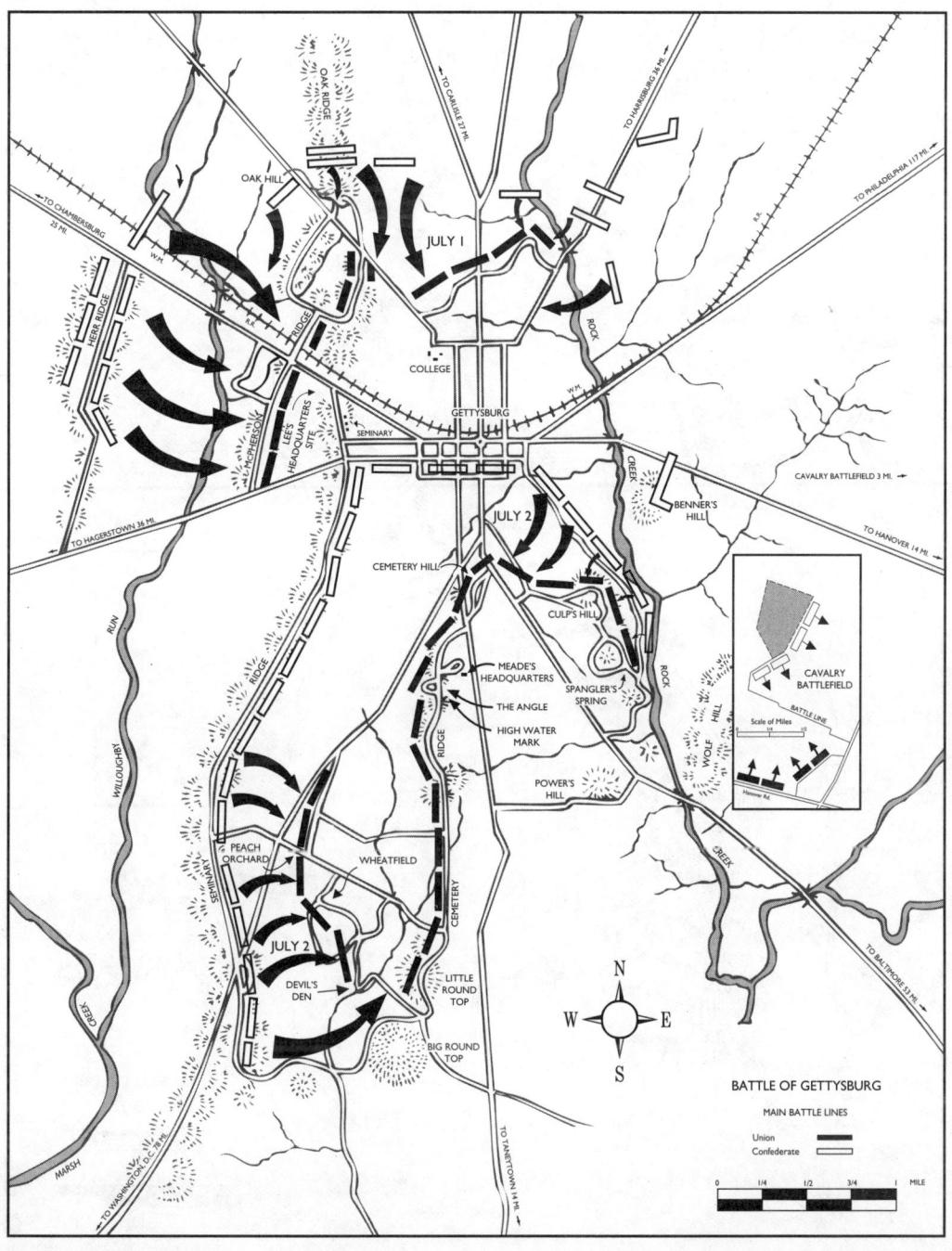

Handout 5

July 3

On the third of July, the Union troops were still holding the high ground along Cemetery Ridge and Culp's Hill. The Rebel troops were massed around the "fish hook." Lee's strategy was to attack the center of the Union line. He ordered Longstreet to fire artillery at the center of the line along Cemetery Ridge. The cannonade began at 1:00 p.m. and lasted for nearly two hours. When the bombardment stopped, nearly 15,000 troops led by General George Pickett, charged more than a half mile across an open field toward the Union troops dug in along Cemetery Ridge. Union forces opened up with artillery fire. The charge continued. The Union forces opened up with more gunfire. When the battle was over, the Union forces had prevailed and the Confederate troops had lost the battle.

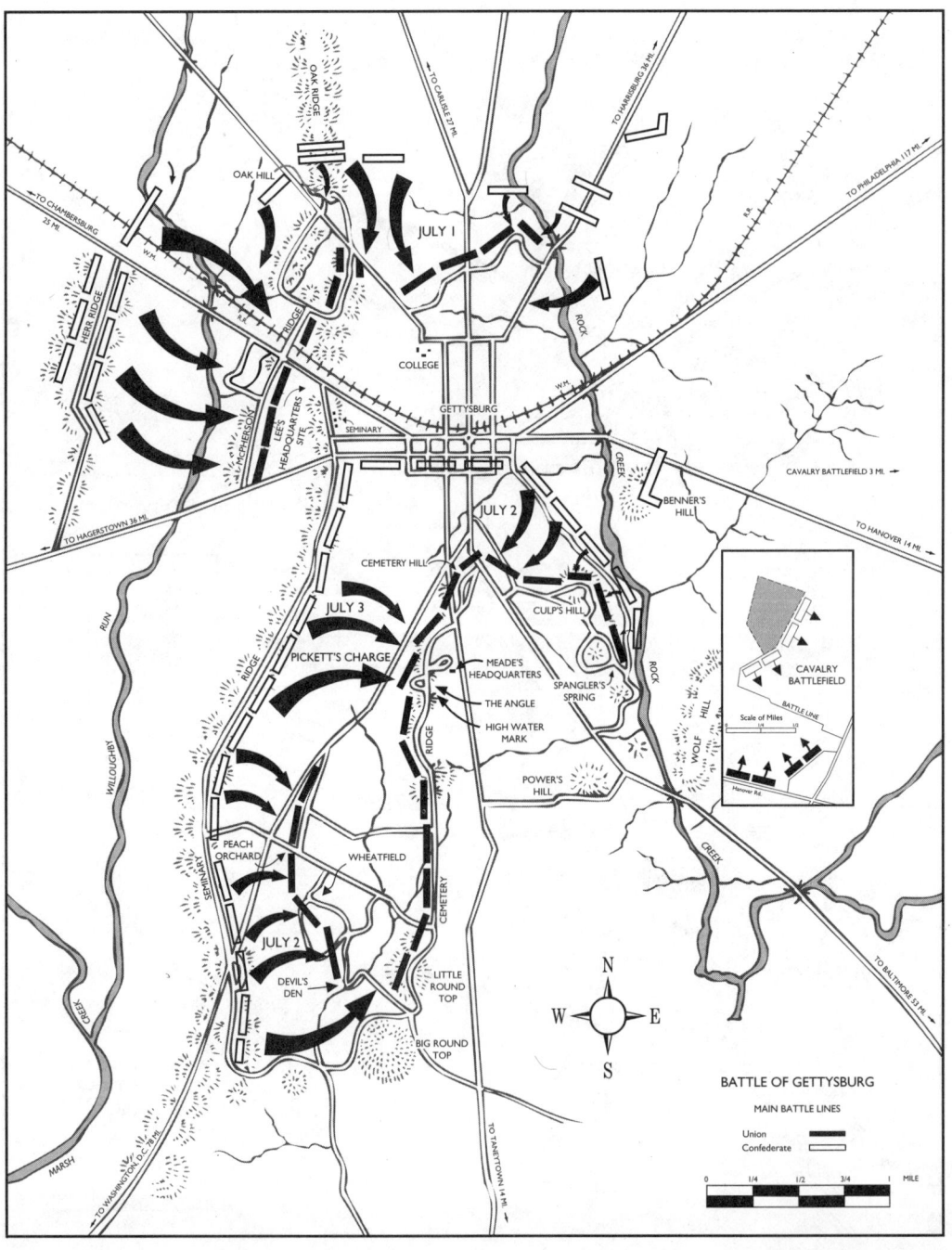

Name _____

Battle of Gettysburg Map

On the map, draw the positions of the Union and Confederate forces and the main battle action of July 2 and 3.

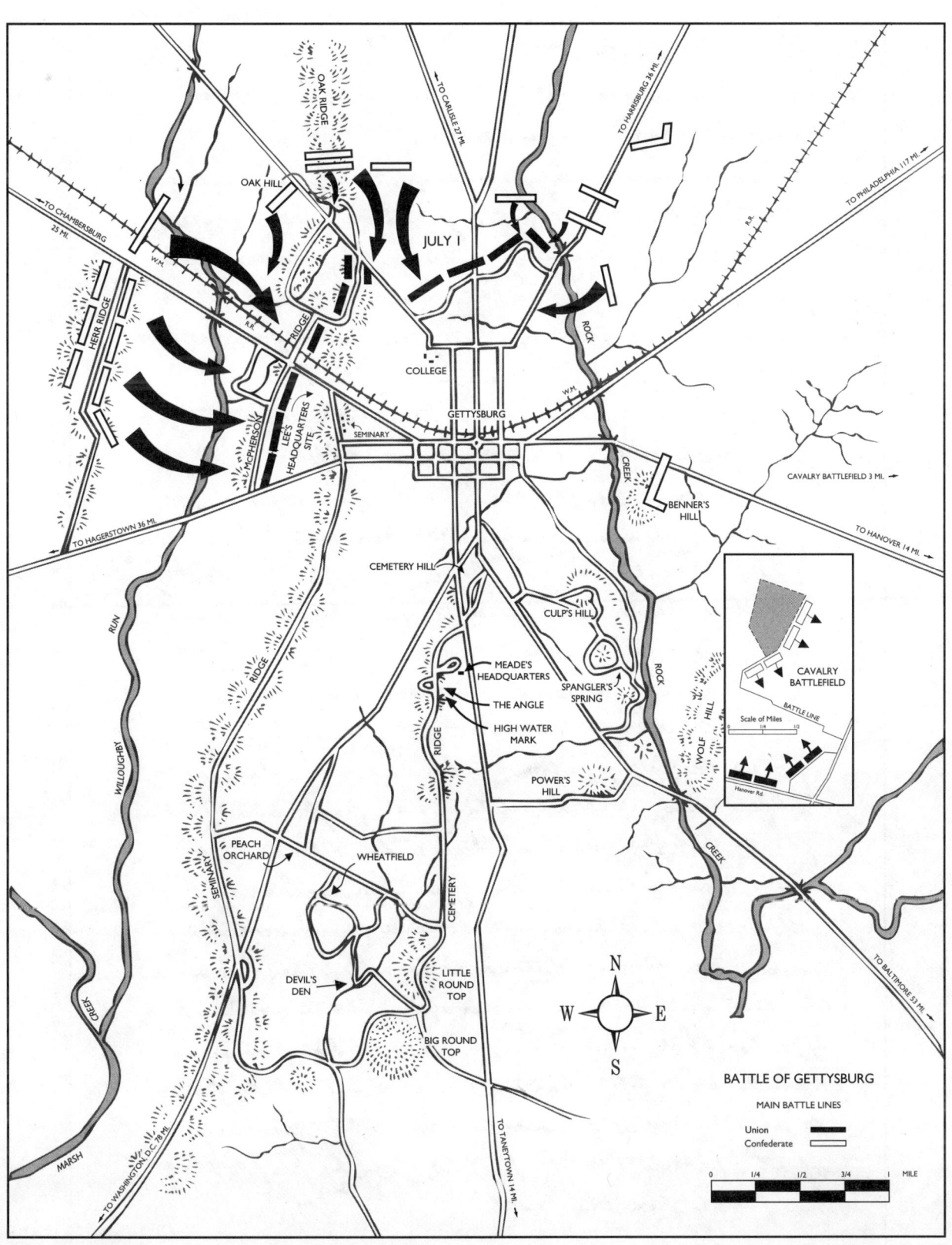

Handout 6

21

Handwritten Version of Gettysburg Address

Below is a copy of Lincoln's Gettysburg Address in his own handwriting.

> Four score and seven years ago our fathers brought forth, on this continent, a new nation, conceived in Liberty, and dedicated to the proposition that all men are created equal.
>
> Now we are engaged in a great civil war, testing whether that nation, or any nation so conceived and so dedicated, can long endure. We are met on a great battle-field of that war. We have come to dedicate a portion of that field, as a final resting place for those who here gave their lives, that that nation might live. It is altogether fitting and proper that we should do this.
>
> But, in a larger sense, we can not dedicate— we can not consecrate— we can not hallow— this ground. The brave men, living and dead, who struggled here, have consecrated it, far above our poor power to add or detract. The world will little note, nor long remember what we say here, but it can never forget what they did here. It is for us the living, rather, to be dedicated here to the unfinished work which they who fought here have thus far so nobly advanced. It is rather for us to be here dedicated to the great task remaining before us— that from these honored dead we take increased devotion to that cause for which they here gave the last full measure of devotion— that we here highly resolve that these dead shall not have died in vain— that this nation, under God, shall have a new birth of freedom— and that government of the people, by the people, for the people, shall not perish from the earth.

Gettysburg Address

Abraham Lincoln spoke these words November 19, 1863, at the dedication of the Soldier's Cemetery at Gettysburg, Pennsylvania.

Four score and seven years ago our fathers brought forth, on this continent, a new nation, conceived in Liberty, and dedicated to the proposition that all men are created equal.

Now we are engaged in a great civil war, testing whether that nation, or any nation so conceived, and so dedicated, can long endure. We are met on a great battlefield of that war. We have come to dedicate a portion of that field, as a final restingplace for those who gave their lives that that nation might live. It is altogether fitting and proper that we should do this.

But, in a larger sense, we can not dedicate—we can not consecrate—we can not hallow—this ground. The brave men, living and dead, who struggled here, have consecrated it, far above our poor power to add or detract. The world will little note, nor long remember what we say here, but it can never forget what they did here. It is for us the living, rather, to be dedicated here to the unfinished work which they who fought here have thus far so nobly advanced. It is rather for us to be here dedicated to the great task remaining before us—that from these honored dead we take increased devotion to that cause for they gave the last full measure of devotion—that we here highly resolve that these dead shall not have died in vain—that this nation, under God, shall have a new birth of freedom—and that government of the people, by the people, for the people, shall not perish from the earth.

Name _____

Understanding the Gettysburg Address

Carefully read Lincoln's Gettysburg Address and answer the following questions. (If necessary, use other resources to answer the questions.)

1. How long is a score? _____

2. Subtract fourscore and seven years from 1863. What year was Lincoln talking about?
   _____

3. What event took place fourscore and seven years ago?
   _____

4. What American document proclaims that "all men are created equal"?
   _____

5. What battlefield is Lincoln's speech meant to dedicate? _____

6. In what war was the battle fought? _____

7. What was significant about this battle? _____
   _____

8. How long did this war last? _____

9. Was Lincoln correct about the world not remembering what he said?
   _____

10. What do the words *government of the people, by the people, for the people* signify?
    _____

Newspaper and Personal Accounts

Read the following accounts of the Lincoln's Gettysburg Address:

Edward Everett

"I should be glad if I could flatter myself that I came as near to the central idea of the occasion in two hours as you did in two minutes."

John Hay

"the President, in a fine, free way, with more grace than is his wont, said his half dozen words of consecration."

Providence Journal

"We know not where to look for a more admirable speech than the brief one which the President made at the close of Mr. Everett's oration ... Could the most elaborate and splendid be more beautiful, more touching, more inspiring, than those thrilling words of the President? They had in our humble judgement the charm and power of the very highest eloquence."

Chicago Times

"Readers will not have failed to observe the exceeding bad taste which characterized the remarks of the President ... at the dedication of the soldier's cemetery at Gettysburg. The cheek of every American must tingle with shame as he reads the silly, flat, and dish-watery utterances of the man who has to be pointed out to intelligent foreigners as the President of the United States."

Harrisburg's Patriot and Union

"We pass over the silly remarks of the President; for the credit of the nation we are willing that the veil of oblivion shall be dropped over them and that they shall no more be repeated or thought of."

Richmond Examiner

"So far the play was strictly classic. To suit the general public, however, a little admixture of the more irregular romantic drama was allowed. A vein of comedy was permitted to mingle with the deep pathos of the piece. This singular novelty, and deviation from classic propriety, was heightened by assigning this part to the chief personage. Kings are usually made to speak in the magniloquent language supposed to be suited to their elevated position. On the present occasion Lincoln acted the clown."

Name _____

Understanding the Newspaper and Personal Accounts

Read the quotes about Lincoln's Gettysburg Address and answer the following questions:

1. The first two quotes about Lincoln's speech were from Edward Everett and John Hay. Who were these two men? How did they know President Lincoln? Were their opinions favorable about the speech? _____

2. Read all the comments about the Gettysburg Address. What did people think about Lincoln's speech? _____

3. Which paper, the *Providence Journal* or the *Chicago Times*, more closely describes your point of view about the Gettysburg Address? Explain. _____
_____

4. The *Chicago Times* was considered a Democrat newspaper. Why might that make a difference? What party did Lincoln belong to? _____

5. Was the *Patriot and Union* correct about the veil of oblivion being dropped over Lincoln's remarks? _____

6. Why would the *Richmond Examiner* be so critical about Lincoln's remarks at the cemetery dedication? (Clue: Find Richmond, Virginia, on a map.) _____

7. What did Lincoln say about the Gettysburg speech in the speech itself? Was Lincoln correct? _____
_____

Discussion Questions

1. How can two opinions be so different about the same speech?
2. Why is it important to understand the point of view of the writer?
3. Should newspapers include opinion?

Further Activities

On the back of this sheet, write an editorial describing your opinion of the Gettysburg Address.

Listen to a speech by a politician on television. On another sheet of paper, write two editorials about the speech. Write an editorial favoring the speech and one that is critical.

26   Handout 11

Political Cartoons

Political cartoons are pictorial editorials. That is, the cartoonist sends a message to the reader with a combination of words and pictures. Quite often the cartoonist will use humor, satire and irony to depict his or her point of view.

Caricatures, drawings of people whose features have been exaggerated, are often used in the political cartoons, too. Well-known symbols are used in every form of medium. Some of the best-known symbols are used in advertising. The cartoonist relies on the reader to understand the symbols in the cartoon. Look at the cartoon here and answer the questions on page 28.

Tennessee State Library

Name _____

Understanding the Cartoon

1. Who is the man on the ball?
   _____

2. How do the tailor's needle and scissors tell the reader who this is?
   _____

3. Who is the man with the split rail?
   _____

4. Why is the split rail used as a symbol with this man in this cartoon?
   _____

5. What does the ball represent?
   _____

6. What are the two men trying to do?
   _____

Beyond the Cartoon

1. On the back of this sheet, draw a cartoon that depicts the same point of view as the cartoon with Uncle Abe and Andy but using different symbolism.

2. Political cartoons employ symbolism. Symbols are used to depict people and parties. Symbols are used in many other aspects of our lives, too, including advertising. When those symbols are used over and over, the symbols become quickly recognizable. What does the symbol of the golden arches make you think of? List three other symbols used in advertising. _____
   _____

3. What does the cartoon character of Uncle Sam represent? _____

4. This cartoon shows a split rail to represent a famous political figure of the day. What animal symbolizes the Republican party? _____

5. What animal symbolizes the Democratic party? _____

6. On another sheet of paper, draw a political cartoon to illustrate your point of view about a current event or issue that is in the news.

Bibliography

Resources for Teachers

Boller, Paul F., Jr. *Presidential Anecdotes.* New York: Oxford University Press, 1981.

Boller, Paul F., Jr. *Presidential Campaigns.* New York: Oxford University Press, 1984.

Kunhardt, Dorothy Meserve, and Philip B., Jr. *Mathew Brady and His World.* Alexandria, VA: Time-Life Books, 1977.

Kunhardt, Philip B., Jr. *Lincoln: An Illustrated Biography.* New York: Alfred A. Knopf, Inc., 1992.

Lorant, Stefan. *Lincoln: A Picture Story of His Life.* New York: Harper & Brothers, 1952.

Sandburg, Carl. *Abraham Lincoln: The Prairie Years.* Volumes I and II. New York: Harcourt, Brace and Company, Inc., 1926.

Sandburg, Carl. *Abraham Lincoln: The War Years.* Volumes I, II, III and IV. New York: Harcourt, Brace and Company, Inc., 1939.

Shaara, Michael. *Killer Angels.* New York: Ballantine Books, 1975.

Wills, Gary. *Lincoln at Gettysburg: The Words That Remade America.* New York: Siman & Schuster, 1992.

Suggested Books for Students

Eifert, Virginia S. *Out of the Wilderness: Young Abe Lincoln Grows Up.* New York: Dodd, Mead & Company, 1961.

Freedman, Russell. *Lincoln: A Photobiography.* New York: Clarion Books, Ticknor & Fields, A Houghton Mifflin Company, 1987.

North, Sterling. *Abe Lincoln: Log Cabin to White House.* New York: Random House, 1956.

Sandburg, Carl. *Abe Lincoln Grows Up.* New York: Harcourt & Brace, Inc., 1926.

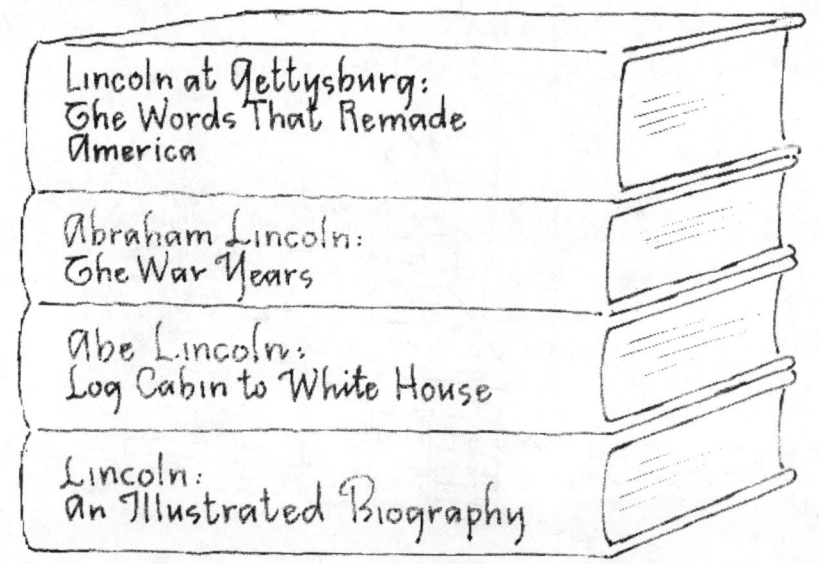
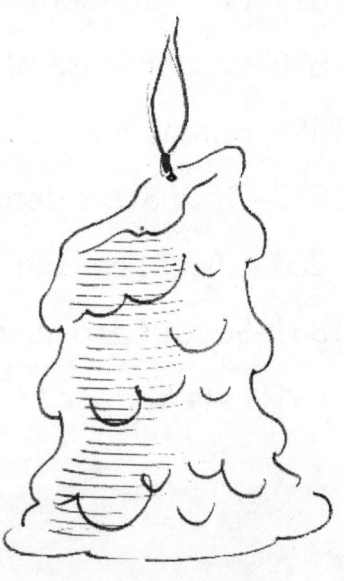

Answer Key

Biography Crossword, page 12

	1R	2E	3P	U	4B	L	5I	C	A	6N
	7A	B	E		O		L			C
	I		O		O		8L	O	9G	
	L		10P	E	T		I		E	
	S		L		H		N		11T	12N
	13P	O	E	T		14S	O	15U	T	H
	L					16C	I	T	Y	
	I		17A	18S			S		S	
	19T	20A	X	L	21A	22W		23A	B	E
	24T	H	E	A	T	E	R		U	
	E			V		E		25O	R	E
	R		26R	E	A	D	I	N	G	

Civil War Time Line, page 16

1808–Constitution outlaws foreign slave trade

1820–Missouri Compromise

1850–Compromise of 1850

1854–Kansas-Nebraska Act

1857–Dred Scott decision

1860–Lincoln elected

1861–South Carolina secedes

1861–Fort Sumter fired on

Answer Key

Battle of Gettysburg Map, page 21

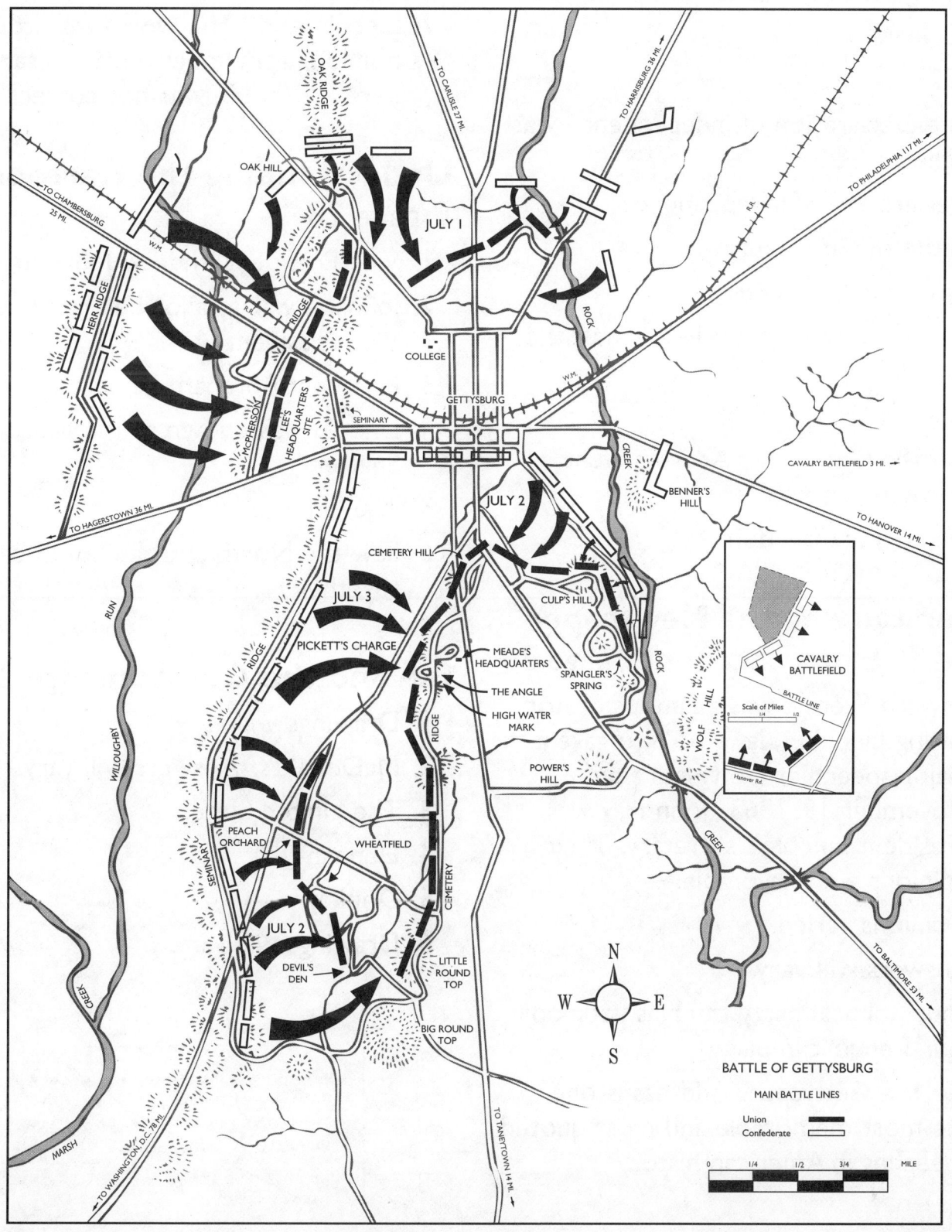

Answer Key

Understanding the Gettysburg Address, page 24

1. 20 years
2. 1776
3. The Declaration of Independence was signed.
4. Declaration of Independence
5. Battle of Gettysburg
6. American Civil War
7. It was a turning point in the war; the North began to win.
8. 1861-1865
9. No, the Gettysburg Address went down in history.
10. Democracy, freedom

Understanding the Newspaper and Personal Accounts, page 26

1. Edward Everett was a famous orator during Lincoln's day who also gave a major speech at Gettysburg on November 19, 1863. John Hay was President Lincoln's secretary. Their opinions were favorable.
2. Opinions varied.
3. Answers will vary.
4. Your political party can bias your opinion. Republican party.
5. No, the Gettysburg Address is one of the most memorable and most quoted speeches in American history.
6. Richmond is in the south, and the South was at war with the North.
7. Lincoln said, "The world will little note, nor long remember what we say here, ..." He was not correct.

Understanding the Cartoon, page 28

1. Vice President Andrew Johnson
2. Johnson was a tailor before he became Vice President.
3. President Abraham Lincoln
4. Lincoln was known as the Illinois Rail Splitter.
5. The Union
6. Sew the North and the South back together

Beyond the Cartoon, page 28

1. Drawings will vary.
2. McDonald's. Answers will vary.
3. The United States
4. Elephant
5. Donkey
6. Drawings will vary.

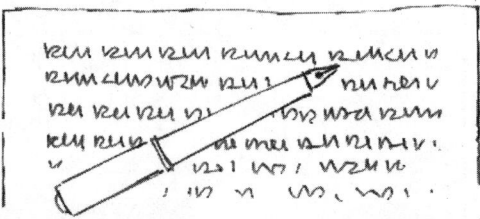